A DINOSAUR DREAM ADVENTURE

WRITTEN BY
J.P. ANTHONY WILLIAMS

DREAM WEAVER TALES

Thank You - Your Free Gift

Thank you for your interest in "A Dinosaur Dream Adventure" You can download your exclusive FREE copy of this amazing Activity Book by scanning the QR code with your phone camera. And don't forget to check out the other Free coloring book at the end of the book.

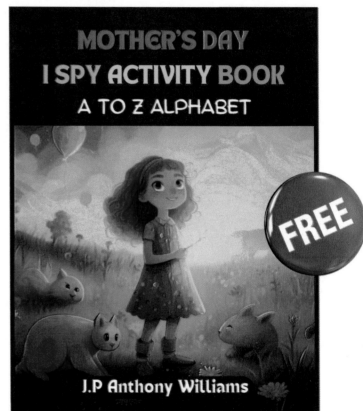

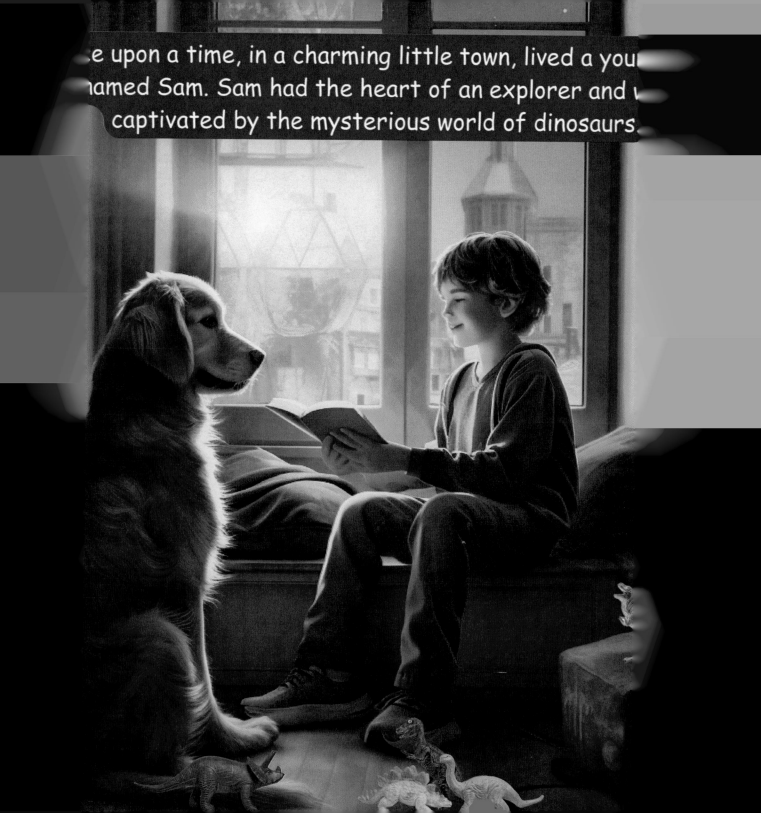

e upon a time, in a charming little town, lived a you
named Sam. Sam had the heart of an explorer and
captivated by the mysterious world of dinosaurs.

Every night, with his loyal dog Spot by his side, he would dive into a book full of tales about dinosaurs before drifting off to sleep.

One night, Sam dreamt he was playing with his dog Spot in his backyard at night.

Spot started sniffing and digging the ground to discover a large egg. It was smooth with a speckled surface shimmering with a hint of hidden wonders.

Sam's eyes widened with wonder.

"Could it be a dinosaur egg?" he wondered aloud. And, as if answering his question, the egg began to shake and crack.

Out of the shell emerged a small dinosaur with bright, playful eyes and a trail of softly glowing scales running down its back.

This was Ross, a baby Brontosaurus!
"Hello, Sam. Hello, Spot," Ross greeted them, his voice soft and friendly.

Ross then revealed something amazing. He had a unique ability to travel through time! "Like to see where I come from, Sam? A time when HUGE dinosaurs roamed Earth. Would you, yes? yes?" Ross said in a funny accent, his eyes sparkling with excitement.

With a nod from Sam, Ross's scales began to glow brighter. In a blink of an eye, they were transported to a lush forest bustling with dinosaurs. Sam was awestruck.

He saw two baby dinosaurs playing hide-and-seek, with their colorful scales harmoniously blending with the lush forest around them.

But Sam's joy was cut short by a sudden shower of meteors lighting up the sky. The dinosaurs started panicking and running around in fear.

"We have to help them, Spot," Sam said, looking worried. Spot barked in agreement, quickly finding a large cave nearby.

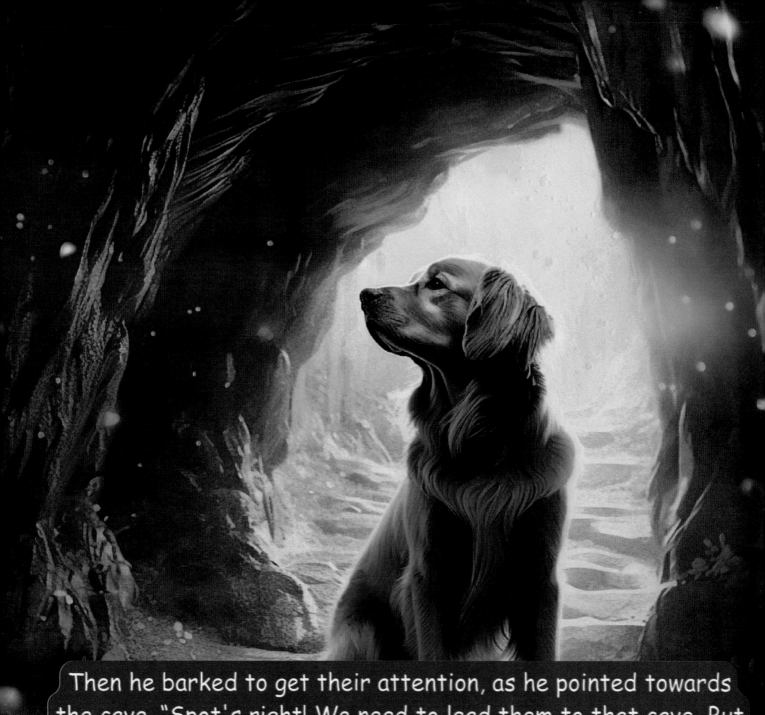

Then he barked to get their attention, as he pointed towards the cave. "Spot's right! We need to lead them to that cave. But how do we get their attention?" Sam pondered.

Sam then had an idea. He lit up a torch ad started waving it, creating a whirlwind of light. The frightened dinosaurs paused, turning their attention towards him. Meanwhile, Ross guided the dinosaurs to the cave.

The dinosaurs began to move towards the cave. "It's working, Ross!" Sam shouted, a broad smile spreading across his face.

Inside the cave, all was calm. The cave shielded the dinosaurs from the meteorites. Sam, Spot, Ross, and the dinosaurs waited together until the shower passed.

"Dank you, Sam and Spot," murmured a grateful Stegosaurus with a funny accent, her voice filled with appreciation. "You us from de dangers of de falling stars saved!"

A Triceratops nodded in agreement. "Yes, safety you guided us. We happy as a T-Rex dancing tango!"

Sam, beaming with pride, turned to Spot and Ross. "They're thanking us! We did it!"

"A team effort, Sam, it was! The power of friendship, we totally showed them, oh yeah! Together, we smash any challenge!" Ross replied with his warm smile and funny accent.

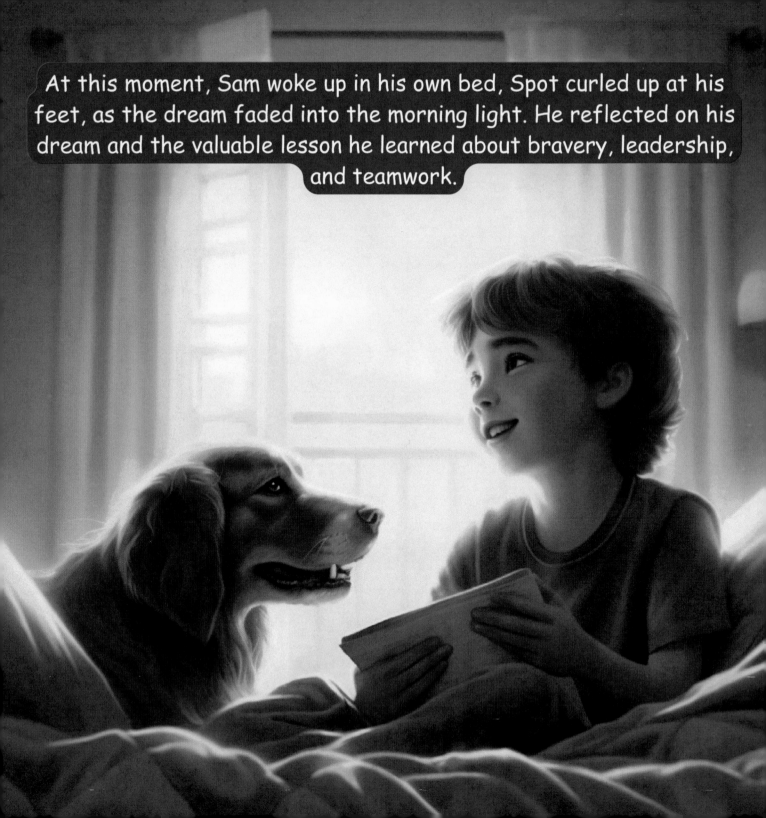

From that day forward, Sam's love for dinosaurs grew even deeper. And every night, he'd dive back into his dinosaur books, Spot by his side; ready for another adventure, and hoping to meet Ross again in

THE END

Check out the other books in this series

Thank You - Your _Free_ Gift

Thank you for reading **"A Dinosaur Dream Adventure"**.

I hope you enjoyed it and if you have a minute to spare, I would be extremely grateful if you could post <u>a short review on my book's Amazon page</u>

To show my gratitude, I am offering a FREE copy of this amazing <u>Animals Coloring Book.</u> Download your free copy by scanning the QR code with your phone

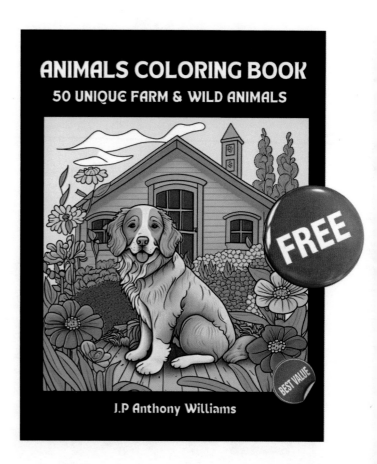

What's Next
Scan QR Code for other Books in this Series

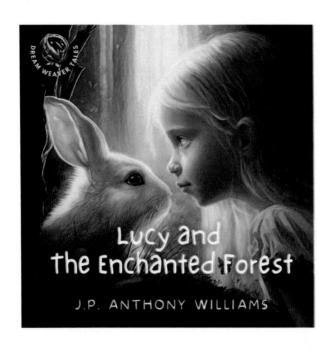

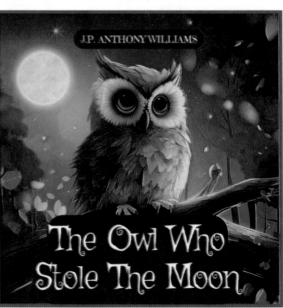

What's Next
Scan QR Code for other Books in this Series

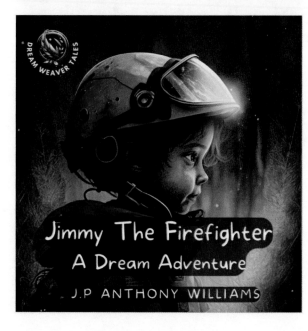

About the Author

J.P Anthony Williams is a bestselling children's book author, known for his enchanting tales and vivid illustrations. His stories are loved by young readers all over the world.

Born and raised in a small town, J.P developed a love of nature and storytelling at an early age. He spent his childhood exploring the woods and fields near his home, and he loved nothing more than curling up with a good book.

J.P's stories are known for their vivid imagery and richly-detailed illustrations. He takes inspiration from the natural world and from the myths and legends of his childhood, and he weaves them into tales that are both entertaining and educational.

In his free time, J.P can be found exploring new places and seeking inspiration for his next book. He is also a big advocate for environmental conservation, and often uses his platform to raise awareness about nature and its preservation.

Special thanks to my wife and kids for their endless support.

Made in the USA
Las Vegas, NV
09 November 2023